*TO MATT, WHO HAS MY HEART
(BUT NO TRUCK)—S. F.*

*FOR MY PARENTS,
AND FOR MY DAD'S "MONSTER TRUCK."—N. H.*

Trucks on Trucks
Text copyright © 2022 by Sorche Fairbank
Illustrations copyright © 2022 by Nik Henderson
All rights reserved. Manufactured in Italy.
For information address HarperCollins Children's Books,
a division of HarperCollins Publishers, 195 Broadway,
New York, NY 10007.
www.harpercollinschildrens.com

The full-color art was created digitally and with gouache paint.
The text type is Antique Olive Std.

Library of Congress Cataloging-in-Publication Data is available.

ISBN 978-0-06-284209-1 (hardcover)

First Edition

22 23 24 25 26 RTLO 10 9 8 7 6 5 4 3 2 1

 Greenwillow Books

TRUCKS ON TRUCKS

BY **SORCHE FAIRBANK**

ILLUSTRATIONS BY **NIK HENDERSON**

GREENWILLOW BOOKS
An Imprint of HarperCollinsPublishers

Blue truck
on red truck.

**Red truck
on blue truck.**

Old truck
on new truck.

**Pink truck
on tow truck.**

Green truck
on no truck.

Bread truck
on red truck.

Pig truck

on big rig truck.

**Fuel truck
on cool truck.**

Small truck.

Medium truck.

Large truck.

Small truck
on medium truck
on large truck.

Dirty truck
on clean truck.

Yellow truck
on green truck.

Bright truck
on white truck.

Dusty truck
on rusty truck.

Clown truck
on brown truck.

Hay truck
      on gray truck.

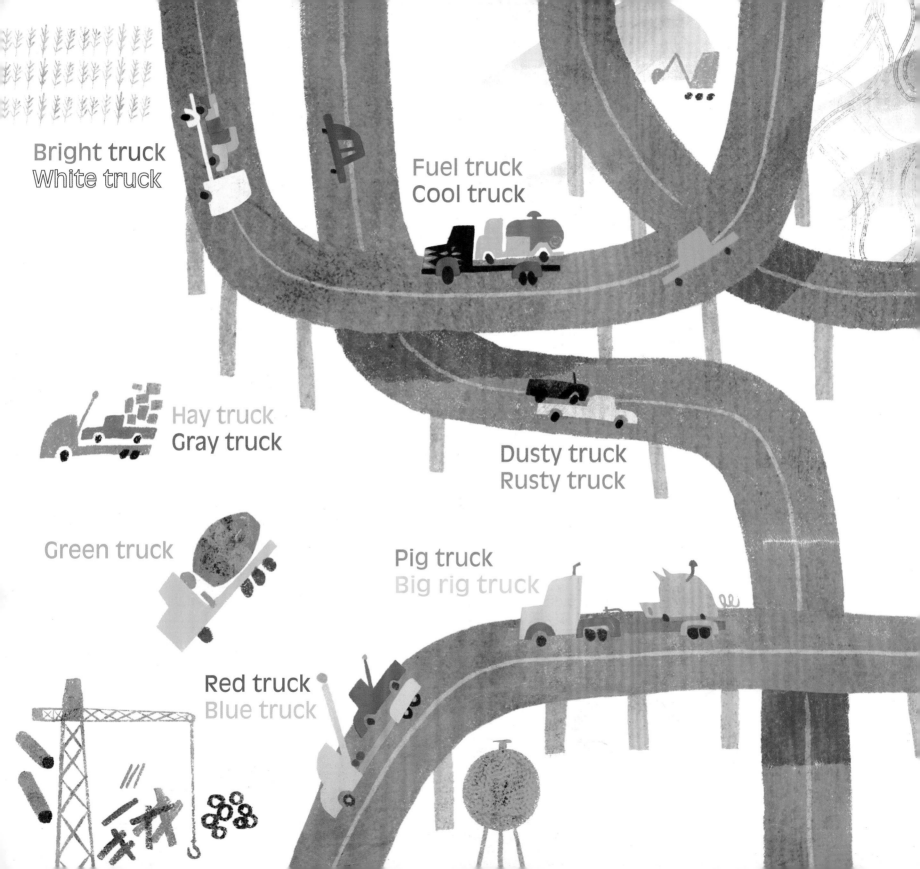

Bright truck
White truck

Fuel truck
Cool truck

Hay truck
Gray truck

Dusty truck
Rusty truck

Green truck

Pig truck
Big rig truck

Red truck
Blue truck

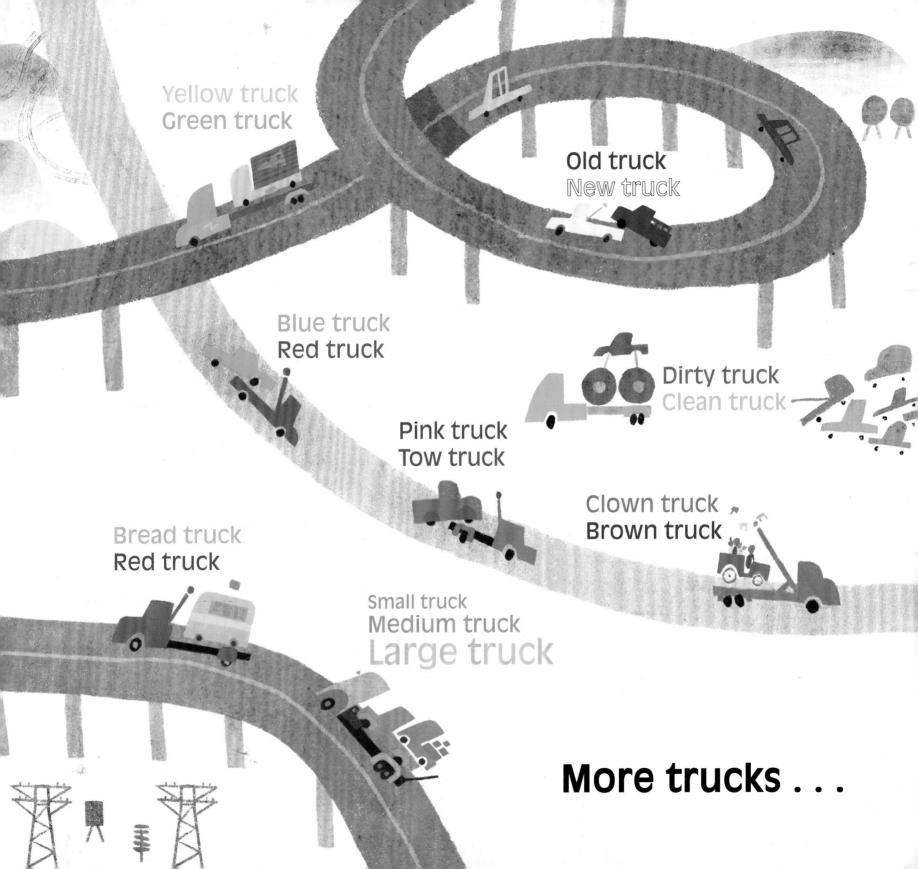

Yellow truck
Green truck

Old truck
New truck

Blue truck
Red truck

Dirty truck
Clean truck

Pink truck
Tow truck

Clown truck
Brown truck

Bread truck
Red truck

Small truck
Medium truck
Large truck

More trucks . . .

Your truck.

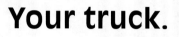

Honk, honk!
VROOM! Vroom!